AN I WISH YOU ALL THE BEST SHORT STORY

I'LL BE HOME FOR CHRISTMAS

MASON DEAVER

ALSO BY MASON DEAVER

ANOTHER NAME FOR THE DEVIL
FOOLS IN LOVE
THE FEELING OF FALLING IN LOVE
THE GHOSTS WE KEEP
I WISH YOU ALL THE BEST
THE (OTHER) F WORD, EDITED BY ANGIE MANFREDI

Book design: Trịnh Hồng Hương
Cover design: Trịnh Hồng Hương
Cover illustration: Alice Oseman

This one is for y'all

DECEMBER 23, 2019

"Okay, I'm pulling in now. Where are you coming out?" Hannah's voice comes in through my phone speaker, though I can hardly hear her with the number of cars and buses honking around me and the roar of airplanes taking off and landing in the distance.

I do not like airports.

It only took my first time flying, four months ago, for me to figure that out. It's not even the whole flying-thirty-thousand-feet-in-a-big-metal-tube-that-most-*certainly*-should-not-be-able-to-fly thing. Though that doesn't help.

It's a lot of the smaller things that spike my anxiety. Like waiting in a line just so a TSA agent can yell at me and convince me I'm doing something illegal that'll land me on a no-fly list. Or how far apart the gates are, and the panic I feel that I'll miss my flight, even though I got to the airport two hours before takeoff.

Or the *people*.

My God, there are so many people traveling for the holidays.

You'd think they'd all want to be home with their families and loved ones. Then again, here I am flying to see my family so… pot calling the kettle black, I suppose.

"I'm at…" I look around for any kind of sign. "D?"

"Was that a question?"

"No…?" I tell her. "Maybe… I don't know."

"Okay…" Hannah huffs, though I can't blame her. There are so many cars out here, lines and lines of people waiting to be picked up. I wouldn't want to be out here two days before Christmas either. And just think, I'd get to do this all again tomorrow. "I think I see you. What is that sweater? I've never seen you wear black before."

I stare down at my chest. "What? It's comfy."

"It's so big."

"It's Nathan's," I say.

"Ohhhhh," Hannah sings. "Wearing Nathan's sweater!"

"Stop." I feel my face getting hot, but I can't resist smiling.

"I'm right here, kiddo." Hannah flashes her flood lights and I avoid nearly getting hit by a car so I can hop in now instead of having to wait for her to pull up. I do only have a backpack with me after all. "Thank God, we can get out of here." Hannah merges with the traffic without really looking, hitting the gas so hard I fall back into my seat.

"Hello to you too," I say, buckling my seatbelt.

"Sorry, but the worst place you can be two days before Christmas is the airport."

"What about Walmart?"

"Okay, fair point," she says. Hannah keeps on with the traffic until eventually we make it out onto the highway, where there's even more traffic waiting for us. "We'd better get used to sitting here."

"It's fine, we've got time."

"When is your flight tomorrow?"

"Noon, but I need to get there early to make sure Ryder will do okay."

"Nathan has no idea, right?"

"Nope," I say with a very satisfied smile. I don't want to brag, but I really feel like I'm going to knock this first Christmas with Nathan out of the park. It just involves taking a fully-grown golden retriever all the way to the other end of the country on an airplane.

No pressure.

I'd been wrestling for *months* with what to get Nathan for Christmas. His birthday had already passed before we started dating, and he'd planned this whole elaborate day together for my birthday in October.

So I needed something big.

Something that I couldn't buy at a store or just make myself.

And Nathan had really missed having Ryder around ever since we moved. I was enormously proud of myself when I thought of the plan at Thanksgiving. It was three solid days where Nathan didn't dare leave Ryder's side and vice versa. Even when we slept, Ryder was nestled right between us, almost kicking me off the bed.

Never thought I'd be competing for my boyfriend's affection with his dog.

Of course, Ryder couldn't come with us to California. Nathan had to live in student housing his first year, and since I decided not to do the whole school thing, I moved in with four other queer-friendly people I found through Twitter.

It was a rough couple of weeks there, when we first moved.

So many new people, in a new space, in a new city, where I didn't have Nathan with me most of the time.

After Thanksgiving I'd finally gotten the courage to ask them about Ryder and him living with us. The monthly dog fee would be mine to take care of, plus the walking, feeding, and cleaning up. But that was all a fair price to pay, knowing that Nathan could come and see Ryder any time he wanted.

"How much did the tickets set you back?" Hannah asks.

"Two seats combined with the pet fees on Christmas Eve? Oh, not much."

"Funny." Hannah reaches over, brushing my hair out of my face. "Your hair's gotten long; I like it."

"I need a haircut," I say. "It's a pain to wash."

"Welcome to my world."

With my hair down to my shoulders, Hannah and I look even more alike than before. And even more like our parents. But I don't want to think about that. I don't want to think about that at all—this is supposed to be a happy visit, even if it's short.

After another hour in traffic, we finally make it back home. I mean, back to Hannah's house.

Can I call this place home? Was it ever really that? I'd only lived here for eight months before I moved away. But it's not like the apartment in Los Angeles feels like home either.

I guess I don't feel like I really have a home.

Hannah and Thomas went all out with the decor: fake reindeer out front, wreaths on every door and window, lights strung up all over the place.

"It's like Santa threw up," I say as we pull into the garage.

"Ha ha," Hannah says, giving me her fakest laugh. "Thomas *really* loves Christmas."

"How many times have you watched *A Christmas Story*?"

Hannah glares at me. "Joke's on you. We don't watch it until the all-day marathon."

"What about *National Lampoon's Christmas Vacation*?"

Hannah looks away quickly and mutters something.

"What was that?" I ask.

"Five, okay? Are you happy? We've watched it five times."

"Seriously?"

Hannah shrugs. "It's Thomas' favorite. And we're watching it again tonight, so you better wipe that look off your face."

"What look?" I grab my backpack and climb out of the car. "I'm totally innocent."

"What time are you getting Ryder?" she asks, resting her hands on the roof of her car.

"Probably tomorrow morning—I've been texting Nathan's mom."

"Okay, so just so you've got a fair warning... Thomas got excited when he found out you were coming."

"Really?"

"And he may have started making an entire Christmas dinner this morning."

"Seriously?"

"He loves the holidays, especially Christmas. You lucked out last year missing it."

I wouldn't exactly call being kicked out of the house "lucky."

"At least you're here this year."

"Yeah, I need to take a shower, that plane left me feeling—"

The second she unlocks the door, the smoke pours out of the doorway, flowing right out the still-open garage door, and the sound of the smoke detectors echoes off the walls.

"All I did was go to check my emails." Thomas is standing in the kitchen, using a baking sheet to fan the smoke out of the open doors that lead out into the backyard. "I don't know what happened."

"I didn't even realize it was possible to burn a chicken this badly..." Hannah stares at the full chicken in the sink, smoke still coming off its very charred skin.

"What happened to the potatoes?" I stare at the counter decorated with the other burnt foods.

"They burnt while I put out the fire in the oven."

"And the green beans?" Hannah asks. They've turned into shriveled black sticks that more closely resemble burnt out matches.

"While I put out the potatoes." Thomas sulks.

"At least the rolls are okay." I pick at one to ease my gurgling stomach. I was too nervous to eat before the flight, so all that's been in my stomach all day is the ginger ale I had on the plane.

Thomas looks at me, and then at the counter. And then he just starts laughing, and then Hannah laughs, and then I start laughing.

Bread never tasted so good.

I don't even know why we're laughing, but I guess that's all you can do when your home is nearly burnt down.

"I'm going to order a pizza."

"I like that idea a lot better," Hannah says, digging under the sink and pulling out a large black trash bag to shovel the food into.

"I'll help."

"No, you go relax. You've had a long day."

"It's fine."

"Ben," she waves me off, "go put your things up. Your room is just how you left it."

Not that there was much to leave behind that was mine... but there is comfort in knowing everything will be mostly the same. Hannah was right about Thomas going all out for the holidays. Despite the mess in the kitchen, the rest of the house is decorated immaculately: tinsel hanging from the stair railing, Santa Clauses and nutcrackers everywhere, a huge tree in the living room, and a homemade gingerbread house on a table in the hallway. I can only tell it's homemade because it looks like someone's taken a few bites from the back where they thought no one would notice.

My room *is* almost entirely the same. Hannah's bought new sheets and curtains, and there's a miniature tree seated in front of the windowsill. My drawings are gone from the walls, as are my bags, my clothes, and the few toys and knick-knacks I collected in the few months before I moved.

It mostly looks like it did this time last year.

Before I came here.

I set my backpack at the foot of the bed and stretch out my legs, my socked feet warm despite the chill of the December day outside. It feels good to be back here, even if it's just for a few hours.

I do miss California, though.

And most importantly, I miss one person in particular.

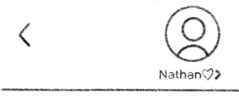

Nathan♡꒳

> I landed and am now safely in the comfort of my old bed.

old bed you say? i miss that thing, we made quite a few memories...

> I'm going to block you, perv.

i was referring to when i made you watch every season of game of thrones in a single month

I still haven't forgiven you for that.

not my fault it fell apart after season four

how was the flight???

Good, bumpy, long...

I read fifty pages of Pride and Prejudice.

and all it took me to get you to read it was whining for six weeks

I'll admit it... it's good.

knew it

How's work?

if I have to make ONE more peppermint mocha I'm gonna cause a scene

i'm never getting the smell off of me

That "yeah." haunts me. Especially that period. I feel like there's so much to unpack.

A whole piece of this plan involved telling Nathan that we wouldn't be spending Christmas Day together. It'd be *super* suspicious if I only came back to North Carolina for a few hours, and I didn't want to give Nathan any reason to think that something might be up.

Unfortunately, that meant him believing that we wouldn't actually get to spend our first Christmas together. Which he was not happy about.

But so long as Nathan got to have Ryder around him all the time, he would forgive me for lying to him. It's just a little white lie after all.

Right?

I throw my hands over my face, my body suddenly filling with dread at the thought of this. Why did I lie to him? I could've just told him the truth or come up with something different. I could've come to get Ryder earlier, but then it wouldn't have been a Christmas surprise. I guess I could've gotten Hannah or Thomas or Sophie or Mel to fly with Ryder, but that'd be unfair.

No.

It'll be okay.

Nathan will totally understand when he sees what I've done.

It'll be fine, it'll be good.

For dinner we order four different pizzas, a box of breadsticks, and a box of cinnamon twists, and lay them all out on the coffee table in the living room; then, Thomas turns on a Christmas movie marathon and we sit back and enjoy the atmosphere, talking to each other, laughing at the movies, eating kinda garbage pizza that still hits different.

It's nice.

It's really nice.

For so long, the holidays were a comfort: spending days with Mom out shopping and helping Dad hang up decorations that'd be left out well into the new year because Mom thought it was wasteful to pack them up the day after.

Then last year happened.

I was so worried that Christmas would lose some of that magic. I still don't know if it has or hasn't yet. There's still this weak feeling in my gut, like something is going to go wrong. Even my medication isn't really helping out much right now. But I'm trying to relax.

I'm sitting here, eating pizza with my family, the new iPad with the Apple Pencil that Hannah, Thomas, and Nathan went all in on for my birthday on my lap, as I try to draw to calm myself down.

Everything is good. It's all good.

So why do I feel so uneasy?

I still carry around a sketchbook with me everywhere I go, along with a pack of pencils and pens, but this thing makes drawing and design way more efficient.

Doesn't hurt that I can just erase my mistakes like they never existed either.

"What are you working on?" Hannah asks, plopping down on the couch next to me.

"Oh, just um…" I struggle to not hide what I'm drawing. "I'm just doodling."

Hannah eyes the sketch of Ryder that I've got pulled up on my screen. "Aw, that's sweet."

"Yeah, just felt like drawing something."

"So, you know I don't have to tell you that owning a dog is a big responsibility, right?"

I sigh. "I know, I know."

"How do your roommates feel about it?"

"They're fine. Most of them were excited about having a pet in the house."

"What's that situation like? Are you comfortable?"

"With my roommates?"

Hannah nods expectantly.

"I mean, yeah. It's fine. A little cramped, but Los Angeles is expensive."

"And you're good on money, right?"

"Yeah, yeah. I'm good."

"Because if you needed help or—"

"Hannah, don't force Ben to take money," Thomas says from the armchair he's bundled in. He's been so invested in the live-action *How the Grinch Stole Christmas* that I don't think he's said a word for the last forty-five minutes.

"I was just being careful; I want Ben to know that we're here for them!"

"It's fine," I tell her loudly enough that Thomas also hears. "I'm fine, I promise."

"You're sure?"

I nod.

"Okay, okay. I just worry about you, kiddo." She pulls me into a tight hug, ruffling my hair. "I want to make sure you're okay."

I feel a swell of warmth. When I moved, I was so worried that Hannah would resent me for it. That she'd basically see it as "thanks for taking me in when I was homeless for a few hours and by the way I'm never paying you back for it *and* I'm moving to the other end of the country—bye!"

Thankfully, that was just my anxiety being mean to me.

That's a mantra I always try to keep in my head, one that Dr. Taylor told me during one of our online appointments.

Anxiety is just a bully.

My feelings aren't facts.

The movie on the TV ends, and Hannah and I both hear sniffles from the other end of the room. We look over to see Thomas sitting there, wiping his eyes with the sleeve of his sweater.

"Is he crying?" I whisper.

"The Grinch really gets to him," Hannah sighs, standing up. She tugs on his shoulder. "Come on, help me clean up."

"His heart grew two sizes… and he saved Christmas…"

"I know, babe. I know…" She pats his back carefully.

I laugh quietly, going back to my drawing as Hannah and Thomas take the empty pizza boxes into the kitchen. I almost wish I were staying for longer, that we'd get to have an actual Christmas together. The only thing we're missing is Nathan and his parents—then it'd be a proper family Christmas. I listen to the credits as they roll, sketching away at this drawing of Ryder that could have probably been its own present so I wouldn't have had to do all of this.

But Nathan's worth the hassle.

I feel like I'd do anything to keep seeing that smile.

But then a notification dings on my phone.

A text.

At first, I think it's got to be from Nathan, but I think he's supposed to be at work still.

555-76 ⟩

555-76: **Dear valued customer, we're sure you're aware of the incoming snowstorm that's expected to make landfall late tomorrow afternoon. Please make sure you've planned accordingly, and if you believe this will impact your flight, please contact us to reschedule.**
Happy holidays.

Snowstorm?

I pull up the Weather Channel app on my phone quickly, looking at the map of the east coast. Sure enough, the rest of this week seems like it'll be decorated in snow.

"Hey, Hannah? Thomas?" I stand up, walking into the kitchen.

The both of them look like they're laughing at something one of them said, bright smiles on their faces.

"What's up, Benji?" Thomas asks.

"Did you see this?" I hold my phone out.

"Is that snow?" Hannah asks.

I nod.

"Oh wow… I knew they said there was a possibility, but it was like 5% chance, max, two days ago."

"Well now it's 100%," I say.

"Let me see?" Thomas takes my phone. "What time is your flight tomorrow?"

"Noon."

"Oh, well you're good." Thomas points to where I'm guessing Raleigh is on the map. "You can see from the animation it's not hitting us until like 2:00 or 3:00. You'll be out of the way by then."

"That won't impact the flight, right?"

"It might delay you by a bit, but it shouldn't be a big deal," Thomas says.

I feel the relief flood my chest. "Whew, okay…"

"It'll be fine," Hannah says, waving off my concerns. If only it were that easy for my brain. "Now come on, we've got presents to open." Hannah claps her hands together, a wild smile on her face. And I breathe, in and out.

It's going to be fine.

Everything will be fine.

DECEMBER 24, 2019

Everything is decidedly not fine.

Because when I wake up the next morning, the entire yard is covered in a thin sheet of white, and there's even more snow still coming from the sky.

Fuck.

I race downstairs, shivering as my feet touch the freezing hardwood floor. It's way colder in here than it was last night. Hannah and Thomas are already seated on the couch, watching the weather, warmed up pizza and cinnamon twists on plates.

"It's snowing!" is the first thing I say to them.

"Yeah." Hannah looks over her shoulder. "It came in quicker than expected."

"Way quicker," Thomas adds.

"What happened?" I ask.

"I guess the wind pushed the cold front in," Thomas says. "This isn't even the worst of it; they're expecting more snow over the next few hours."

"Jesus…" I perch on the arm of the couch. "What does this mean?"

Hannah sighs. "I hate to tell you, Benji, but you might be stuck here for Christmas."

"That can't happen," I say.

"I don't know what to tell you, kiddo. I doubt any flights are leaving out for the rest of the day. Has yours been cancelled?"

"I haven't checked…" That's when I realize I left my phone upstairs. It's only had time to charge half-way because I was up until 3:00 FaceTiming Nathan. We'd talked about his day and work and then decided we were going to watch a movie together. I thought it'd make me feel better, but it only made his absence feel that much heavier.

I log in with my flight information and wait for my ticket to load.

"It still says my flight is scheduled for takeoff at noon," I say when I'm back downstairs.

"Well that's not happening." Hannah stands up, taking her and Thomas' nearly empty plates into the kitchen.

I follow her closely. "What do you mean?"

"It's dangerous out there, Benji. You're not leaving this house."

"I don't have a choice. I've got to get back to Nathan."

"No, you don't. Nathan and Ryder can both wait. We'll just reschedule your flight."

"I don't think I can reschedule." I'd grabbed one of the cheap tickets, so unless the flight was flat out cancelled, I'd be out two hundred unbelievably valuable dollars if I missed this flight. "I'm not going to miss Christmas with him."

"Benjamin De Backer, it is not safe," Hannah says firmly. She rarely ever uses my full name, so this is serious. "We'll buy you another ticket, but I'm not having you fly in a blizzard."

"Hannah… I'm not going to miss my first Christmas with him. If you don't take me to the airport, then I'll just get an Uber."

"You won't be able to find an Uber right now."

"Then I'll walk, it's only a ten-minute drive. How far can it be?"

Hannah can't help but laugh, shaking her head as she blasts the dishes with hot water. "You're so stubborn, you know that?"

"I get it from you." I lean over the counter. "Hannah… I'm not missing my first Christmas with Nathan. It's not happening. I'm going to be on that flight, whenever it takes off."

Hannah looks at me, and then down at the sink before she begins mopping up some of the mess she's made with the water with a dish towel.

"Have you talked to Nathan's parents yet?"

"No."

"Fine," she sighs. "Go grab Ryder. We'll drop you off."

I breathe out finally. "Thank you."

"I don't like this plan; I want that on the record."

"Noted."

"Now go get your boyfriend's dog."

If the airport two days before Christmas is hell, then the airport on Christmas Eve is another level below that.

I don't really know what below hell would be.

Mega hell?

Is that a thing?

Either way, the amount of people flying today combined with the snowstorm closing off many of the drop-off lanes means that we sit in traffic for a whole hour before I get close enough to get out.

"How were Nathan's parents?" Thomas asks from the passenger seat.

"Good. They weren't happy that I'm still flying out."

"Oh really?" Hannah glares at me. "Any chance you'll listen to them over your big sister?"

I smile at her. "Nope, not at all."

"Figures."

"It's going to be fine," I tell her.

"Have they delayed you at all?" Thomas reaches toward the backseat, giving Ryder a quick pat on the head.

I check my phone again. "By half an hour." Which is fine by me considering I'll be booking it with Ryder to the gate. And as if he can read my mind, the golden retriever huffs next to me, setting his head in my lap. I reach under his ears, massaging carefully. Maybe he's as anxious as I am. Or maybe he's only anxious because of me. I feel like I read somewhere that animals are better at sensing anxiety than humans are.

"You've got everything for him, right?"

"Yeah, Nathan's mom even had a coat for him to wear."

"That's cute."

I fasten it on to him carefully the closer we get to the drop-off area. The traffic directors are yelling at cars to keep it moving as people say their goodbyes.

"Sorry the visit was so short."

"It's okay, you've got a boyfriend to get back to."

"We'll come and visit soon, the both of us. When Nathan gets time off from work."

"You grabbed his present, right?" Hannah asks.

"Yeah. It's in my bag."

"Good."

We finally pull up to the curb and I grab my bag, giving Hannah and Thomas the most awkward hugs of my life from the backseat before I drag Ryder out of the car. Poor dude probably could've done with a nice pair of boots to protect his paws from the chill.

"I love you two."

"Love you," Hannah says.

Thomas waves. "Love you, Ben!"

"Please call us if your flight is delayed or cancelled! We'll come get you."

"I will, I promise!" I wave to them both, leading Ryder into the warmth of the airport terminal. If being on your own in an airport is overwhelming and stressful, try adding a dog that wouldn't pee before you left the house and who is bound and determined to sniff everything in sight.

Maybe I should've gotten a crate.

But that just seemed wrong.

"Ryder, buddy." I call him closer, putting my hand under his chin. "You've got to behave, okay? For me and Nathan, alright?"

He sticks his tongue out, but something in his expression tells me he's listening.

Or maybe I'm just making things up.

"I'm going to find you one of those pet rooms before we stand in TSA for an hour."

Ryder follows me closely, and I try to keep a hand on both his head and his leash, leading him with both. Despite a rough start, Ryder eases into being at the airport. He stays beside me the entire walk to the pet-safe room where they have those patches of fake grass for him to pee on—which, thankfully he does, so that's one less thing to worry about.

I didn't want Ryder to have to hold his bladder for five straight hours on a direct flight to Los Angeles, so I grabbed one with an hour layover in Dallas. Which was harder to find than I thought it'd be.

So many flights just wanted to take me to Atlanta, and a few wanted to take me all the way to Ontario for some reason.

"You good?" I ask Ryder as we stand in line. I catch a few looks, some people awwing at Ryder and his majesty, waving hello at him, or trying their best to give him a scratch behind the ears before we move too far away.

Other people are glaring at me, as if having a dog is the worst inconvenience in the entire world for some reason.

People are so annoying.

We finally make it to the front of the line, and we're told to step to the side since we're a special case. Someone comes by and pats Ryder down, which he thinks is an invitation to lick the TSA agent.

Thankfully, they don't mind, and they give him a swift pat on the head when they're done.

"He's trained well," the agent tells me.

"Thanks, he's my boyfriend's."

"That's sweet." I don't see a weird look in their eyes. Maybe being in California for a few months got me too comfortable talking about my queerness, but I'm not going to go back now. I went through so much to feel comfortable with myself—other people's discomfort with who I am is no longer my problem.

It's theirs.

"We'll need to pat you down too," the agent says.

"Seriously?"

"It's procedure. Do you prefer a male or female agent?"

"Is this necessary?"

"Let's just do it, kid. Don't make a fuss."

Suddenly I like this agent a lot less. "Female, please."

That earns me a strange look. I wonder what it means that I had to choose the gender of the agent. How am I presenting myself today? I guess I'm pretty femme, with my nails painted, hair pulled back, Nathan's oversized sweater that pools around the palms of my hands. I didn't want to put too much effort into my appearance for a seven-hour journey back home.

Another agent comes by. I spread my legs and arms, and feel the discomfort seep into my body. Maybe I'm more confident in some ways, but the only person I want touching me like this is Nathan.

"He's good," the agent says.

"They," I correct.

"Um… okay?"

"Come on, Ryder." I grab my backpack and take his leash, leading him over to the screen that's displaying our flight information. It's right by a window that looks out onto a very white tarmac, where trucks are working to pour what I'm guessing is salt and other chemicals, and people are shoveling the piles and piles of snow that just keep coming down.

I look down at Ryder and he stares at me with those big brown eyes of his.

"Don't worry," I assure him. "We'll make it, I promise."

He sticks his tongue out and does that very doggy smile thing where he obviously doesn't know what's going on but he's simply happy to be a part of the situation.

"Come on." I lead him towards our gate, taking a seat near the windows, where it's less crowded.

There's already a line of people at the kiosk, and the flight attendants attending to everyone look stressed out of their minds.

Actually, everyone looks pretty stressed out. Some business looking person in a suit is on the phone, reprimanding someone in an incredibly low voice; there's a mom consoling her crying child by trying to feed them their snacks; a group of teenagers is huddled in the corner, scrolling through the phones, sad looks on their faces.

I guess we're all having a pretty fantastic Christmas Eve.

Maybe this was a bad idea...

Ryder comes closer, putting his head on my lap.

"Hey, buddy. How are you doing?"

He doesn't answer of course, but his tail starts wagging harder when I put my hand on his head.

"You know your dad missed you. He's been so sad since he moved."

I feel his soft fur on the palm of my hand and move to his belly to unbuckle his coat, stuffing it in my backpack.

"I wonder what that says about him, that he'd miss you more than he misses me. But he probably misses me too... I miss him. You miss him too?"

Ryder's tail just wags harder and harder.

"Yeah, me too."

We'll make it home. We may be late by an hour or so, but we'll make it there. I've got to believe that we will or else I don't know what I'm going to do with myself. I've just got to occupy my brain, and they'll be calling for us to board before too long. I just know it.

"Come on, buddy." I pat the seat next to me. There are no arm rests on these benches, so Ryder should be able to lay down. "You just get some rest; it'll be a long flight."

He climbs up beside me, still putting his head as close to me as he can. I wonder what's going through that head of his, if he knows what's happening, if he's heard Nathan's name enough to realize that he'll be seeing Nathan in just a few hours. The only trouble is that he has to get on a plane to do it.

It probably would've been safer to drive a car all the way to North Carolina, but I would've had to rent one, and that's a ton of gas money. Plus, motel stays for when I'd have to take a break from driving.

And honestly, I don't know what's sadder than a solo road trip just a few days before Christmas. I guess the return trip back with only a dog to talk to is pretty sad to most people too.

I pull my iPad out of my bag and start on another drawing. I don't have anything in my head, so I just start sketching the people that I see around me, some of them seated at other gates. A man with a hot coffee he's delivering to a boyfriend or husband; this teenager with headphones around their neck, music blasting so loud I can hear it from here; the two girls folded into each other, one of them sleeping while the other plays with her hair.

There is such a collection of people here, the options feel unlimited.

And yet so limiting at the same time.

Every few minutes, I find myself staring up at the screen behind the kiosk. There's a firm 12:30 lit up, but with every second we get closer and closer to that time, and it feels like it'll be impossible to meet it.

I look around again at the people surrounding me, the sheer number of folks who are flying to Dallas for one reason or another. If this were a Hallmark movie, we'd all join together and sing Christmas carols while we waited for the blizzard to clear up.

And it would, just in the nick of time. Everything would be okay, I'd get Ryder to Nathan, and we'd have the most magical Christmas together.

The only problem with that is that life isn't a movie.

The time on the screen changes from 12:30 to 1:00.
And then from 1:00 to 1:20.
Then from 1:20 to 1:40.

I sit there and watch everyone else's reactions as the new time comes up, so much hope lost in just a few spare seconds.

"You stay right here, buddy," I tell Ryder as I loop his leash through the hole in the back of his seat. "I'll be right back."

He's still perfectly within view from the line at the kiosk, so he's not going anywhere. There are three people in front of me, and I have a feeling that each of us is here to ask the same question.

One of the flight-attendants has the same intuition.

"Are you all here asking about the flight?"

Me and the person in front of me stand in silence, nodding. The person at the very front of the line speaks up. "Please, my family is waiting for me in Dallas. Isn't there any update you can give me?"

"I'm sorry, sir, but the storm moved too quickly and we weren't prepared. We're waiting to get more salt on the runway."

"I saw a plane land ten minutes ago!"

"I know, sir. They were already in the air before the storm, and they didn't have anywhere else to stop. If it makes you feel any better, that plane and any passengers with connecting flights are grounded here, the same as you."

"I'd like to speak to a manager."

"Sir, I apologize for the inconvenience, but what is it that you think my manager will be able to do about a blizzard that's frozen the runways?" Her tone switches from the light, polite one most customer-service people are expected to use to hard and tired. I can only imagine how difficult this whole blizzard has been for the airport staff.

"I..."

"Please take a seat, all of you. We'll be keeping you updated on the status of your flight. If you're here to cancel, then we can handle that as well and issue you a credit for a later date."

Should I just do that? Call Hannah, ask her to come and pick me up, and make my way to Nathan later this week when the snow is long gone? I pull up the weather app on my phone and take a look at the map, I don't really know what any of it is supposed to mean, but if I have my locations correct, then the storm should be passing us in an hour or two.

Then that just leaves the runways thawing out.

Can that really take that long?

No.

I'm not even going to entertain the idea that I won't make it to Nathan. Everything is going to be fine.

It will be.

I just know it.

I go back to Ryder, rubbing the top of his head. It seems to calm him down just as much as it does me.

Then my phone starts to ring, and Nathan's name lights up on the screen. He's FaceTiming me.

Perfect.

"Stay quiet, okay?" I look at Ryder, plugging in my headphones and hoping that Nathan doesn't know enough about the Raleigh-Durham Airport to place where I am.

"Hey, babe," I answer.

Nathan's angle is weird at first, but then I realize that he's horizontal, still laying in his dorm bed, his sheets pulled up to his chin, hair slightly messy.

"Hey, is everything okay? I saw on the news there was this blizzard where you are."

"Oh, yeah." I try to keep the camera close so he can't see any of the background. "It's pretty bad."

"Where are you?"

"At Thomas and Hannah's, why?"

"I just hear a bunch of people."

And of course, that's the moment the intercom comes on. I mute myself quickly, mouthing words so it looks like I'm talking.

"Ben, baby, I can't hear you."

I feel awful.

I feel like a jerk for lying to him like this. Even if it's an okay lie, one that's for a good reason, I can't escape the dirty feeling it's filling me with. I spent way too long lying to Nathan about who I am, and I don't want to lie again. I mean, this is different, but is it really?

I lied to Nathan about my identity because I feared what he'd think of me. But what will he think of me if I can't even make it back to him for Christmas?

I unmute. "Sorry, bad signal."

"It's okay," he says, though the tone in his voice makes me feel like it's anything but. "I miss you."

"I miss you too."

I'm an asshole.

"But I'll be there soon."

"I know."

"Do you have work today?"

Nathan nods. "I managed to get the morning shift, so I won't have to close."

"You should get out of bed."

"I don't wanna," he whines, burying his face in his pillow.

"If you don't get that paycheck, how can you be my sugar daddy?" I ask.

Nathan lets out a fake gag. "Don't say that, I'm no one's sugar daddy. Not on fourteen dollars an hour."

"Yeah, no. I feel like I need a shower now."

Nathan smiles at me, his brown eyes shining in the morning light. The one singular window in his dorm room lets in the best light in the morning. On the occasions I've been able to sneak sleeping over, I always wake up looking at him washed in yellow, his skin bright, freckles like a constellation dotting his cheeks. Nathan's already beautiful, but there are still so many moments where I'm struck by just *how* gorgeous he is.

And how lucky I am.

Like the way he smiled when we first painted his nails a bright sunflower yellow, or when he brings me coffee from work that he made himself, even though I know he's exhausted and the idea of making anymore coffee must make him sick.

That coffee always tastes the best.

Sometimes I wonder what I did to deserve someone like Nathan Allan in my life. Whatever it was, it certainly wasn't enough. I could live a hundred lifetimes of being nothing but a charitable saint and still never deserve Nathan.

"Seriously, though," I say. "You should get up. I don't want you to be late."

"I know."

"I love you."

"I love you too." He smiles at me, and it's that awkward moment where neither of us wants to end the call, because neither of us want this moment to end.

It's so sappy.

But I love him.

I love him so much.

"Okay, I've actually got to go. I spent too long in bed."

"You mean you don't want to FaceTime while you're in the shower?"

"No unless you want to." Nathan does this fake lip bite with just enough fuckboy energy to make me go red.

"Shut up."

He laughs. "I'll see you soon."

"Okay."

"Love you."

"Love you too."

He ends the call this time, and I stare down at my phone where his face used to be. I wonder if it's healthy to miss a person this much. We've only been officially dating for half a year, but with Nathan, everything is so easy. It's the exact same way it was before prom night, when we found ourselves on the roof. With just as much hand holding, and even more kissing.

I don't have to hide any part of myself from him, and he doesn't have to hide anything from me. I know people think all the time that high school relationships don't last, that it's irresponsible to think that you'd find your soulmate so young, that you should get more experience with different relationships...

But with Nathan, everything feels right. So natural and easy.

I feel like I don't have to try, and that makes me want to try even harder to make sure he's happy.

Maybe that's why I feel so bad right now.

Because I know he's unhappy.

And I know it's because of me.

I look down at Ryder, and he just stares at me, the bottom half of his face hidden by his paws.

"Need to go to the bathroom?"

He perks up, tail wagging, so I'm taking that as a yes.

"Good. I've got to stretch my legs."

I find the nearest room for Ryder to pee in. It's while I'm standing there watching him pee on the pad of fake grass that

I really start to wonder how you'd clean something like this. Or if it even *is* cleaned…

It must be.

Right?

I mean it's not just pee that these things get caught under.

I take a step off the fake grass, back on to the marble-tiled floor in front of the entrance. After Ryder's done, we take a walk through the airport close to our gate. I stop at the Panera and grab a cheese Danish, bottle of water, and two empty bowls, and head back to our old seat. Miraculously still empty.

"Here you go, buddy. Sorry about the wait.

I wasn't worried about Ryder needing to eat much on the flight, but I still asked Mr. Allan if he could pack a small Ziploc bag of some dry food, just in case.

Guess my gut was right.

And another look at the kiosk tells me the flight has been delayed again. There are no flight attendants around this time. I guess they finally got tired of people asking them what's going on.

Then my phone dings.

Mariam ⟩

I forget, what time was I supposed to get you?

Wait, you're in the air. Duh.

> Unless you got shitty plane wi-fi. In which case...

> 1. Why?

> B. Hi!!!!!!! Send Ryder pics.

I laugh at the chaotic energy that six simple texts hold and snap a quick picture of Ryder as he drinks some water.

> BABY!!!!!!!!!!!!!!!!!!!!!!!!

> That's the airport...

> Have you not taken off?

> Nope.

> You can thank this thing...

2:30 PM Tue Dec 24

EMERGENCY ALERT
WINTER STORM

Winter Storm Makes Landfall Earlier Than Expected

December 23, 2019

Yikes.

Does Nathan know?

He knows about the storm, but I didn't tell him about the plan...

Oof.

What are you going to do?

Sit here and wait for the flight time to stop being delayed.

Something about the runways freezing over, I don't know.

Maybe you should go back to Hannah's? Nathan will still be there when you can finally get out.

No.

I don't want to miss my chance.

So you'll risk dying in a frozen plane crash just to see your boyfriend again?

Gay.

Very.

My texts vanish as Mariam starts up a Facetime call.

"Are you sure you shouldn't just go home?" they ask when I answer.

"I don't want to miss whatever chance I might get."

"Benji, Nathan's going to understand."

"I don't want to miss our first Christmas. It's important."

"Christmas is overrated," they say. "Everything smells like peppermint or fake cinnamon, and you can't walk inside anywhere without hearing Christmas songs."

"Yeah, I love it."

Mariam brushes me off. "Whatever, Elf on the Shelf."

"I hate Elf on the Shelf," I tell them.

"There's nothing I can do to convince you to go back to your sister's house, is there?"

I shake my head. "Nope."

"Figures."

"You asked."

"Just be careful, okay?"

"I will, I promise."

"You're not allowed to die on me."

"Who would do the art for our videos if I did?"

"I'm sure I could find someone," Mariam chuckles. "But I'd rather not have to hunt for another artist."

"I'll be fine."

"Okay, Benji."

"I'll call you when I've finally landed."

"Any time, okay? Even if it's 4:00 in the morning, I'll come and grab you."

"Thank you."

"No thanks needed; you're treating me to KBBQ when the holidays are over."

"Fair enough."

A notification flashes on my screen, pausing the call.

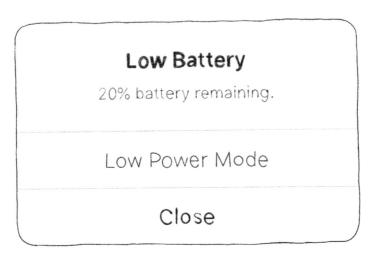

Low Battery

20% battery remaining.

Low Power Mode

Close

"Shit," I mutter.

"What?"

"My phone's dying."

"You have a charger?"

"Yeah, just got to find a place to charge it." A quick glance around the gate tells me that every outlet is filled, either by phone or laptop chargers.

"I'll let you go. Call me if you need me, love you!"

"Love you too."

Mariam ends the call, and I dig around in my backpack for my charger. Thankfully, Ryder finished his food and water, so I can toss the bowls away easily. "Come on, buddy. We're going for a walk."

Ryder follows on his leash, looking around at all the new people, making their way to their gates, where they're probably going to sit for a few hours. I look wherever I can. There are so many gates in this area, so many rest areas, and yet all their outlets filled.

"Is everyone's phone dead?" I ask Ryder, which I guess is the same thing as asking no one.

Finally, after walking for ten minutes, I find one of those long charging bars in the middle of the airport, with exactly one free seat open. Ryder and I both race to reach it, and I plug in my charger swiftly before I even take the seat.

I open up my phone, going to Instagram on autopilot. I scroll through the new likes and comments, eventually going to my own profile where it's mostly pictures of Nathan and me together, a few updates on videos, events, talks, and some art. You can most definitely notice the difference between this time last year, when I had maybe 20 followers, most of them bots, and now after working with Mariam, when my follower count has gotten to the five-digit mark and people share my work constantly.

It's weird.

I won't lie, sometimes I do miss the anonymity.

Sometimes.

"You okay?" I ask Ryder.

He huffs, laying on the carpeted floor.

"Yeah, me too." I look at my phone again, scrolling through my texts. I should call Hannah, give her an update.

"Benji, is everything okay?" is the first thing she asks me when she picks up.

"Yeah, yeah... we're still at the airport."

"Still? Has the flight been cancelled?"

"No, just delayed."

"Ben..." Hannah pauses. She doesn't even have to finish her sentence.

"I'm not leaving, Hannah."

"Please?"

"The flight keeps getting delayed, which means they must

think they'll be able to take off."

"Or they just don't want to refund a ticket and lose money, so they're willing to put passengers' lives at risk."

Yeah, that's probably more accurate.

"I don't want to risk missing the flight."

"You can go in a few days, when this has cleared up, Ben; it's not that big of a deal."

"Maybe to you," I tell her. "It's our first Christmas together. I don't want to miss this."

Hannah lets out a long sigh. "Ben, it's going to be okay… this isn't worth risking your safety over."

Maybe Hannah doesn't get it, but I need this year to be normal. After what happened last year.

"Not getting to spend your Christmas together isn't a big deal, I—" Hannah stops short of her sentence. "Yeah, it's Ben… No, they're not listening to me."

She must be talking to Thomas.

"Yeah, here. Talk to them."

Hannah passes the phone off and my hunch is proven right.

"Ben, hey, what are you doing?"

"Waiting at the airport."

"No, I mean *why* are you still there? We should come and get you."

I don't need this from Thomas as well. "I'm not leaving, not unless the flight is cancelled. And even if it is, I can just book another one."

"Ben, I feel like this is a bit unreasonable."

The worst part is that I know I'm being selfish and petulant, but they just don't understand. "I can't give this up, Thomas. Not after last year. I… I need this."

Thomas goes quiet for so long that I have to double check to make sure the call didn't just drop. That'd be icing on the

37

cake, stuck at the airport with no cell service.

"I get what you mean, Ben. I really do."

"Yeah?"

"But your safety is more important."

I have to ignore the temptation to call him "Mr. Waller."

"Thomas."

"Did Hannah ever tell you that we missed our first Christmas together?"

I pause. "No, she didn't."

"I went to go spend Christmas with my family, and Hannah was stuck at school. She said she wanted to study but we'd already had finals, so I think she was just afraid to meet my family." Thomas lets out a low laugh. "But we still talked to each other every single day, and when I got back to school, we had our own little Christmas together. I mean, it was like the fifth of January, but that's beside the point."

I feel myself smiling.

"The *actual* point is that it's not these holidays that make things special—it's the two of you, and the moments you choose to spend together. You two are going to make so many more memories that before you know it, this first Christmas won't matter."

"I... I know that. I do."

But do I? I'm still here at the airport, and I don't know if I feel like leaving. Not yet.

"Will you let us come and pick you up?"

I take a look around the airport, looking at all the people still stuck here on layovers or waiting for their rides, wishing that they had the chance to go home and not spend Christmas stuck in an airport.

But if this many people have stayed, maybe there's a hope that this will all be over soon?

"I have to stay," I tell Thomas. "At least for a little bit longer."

I can definitely feel Thomas' disappointment through the phone. "Okay, but you'll call us the *second* the flight is cancelled, right?"

"Yeah, I will."

"Okay, Benji… we love you."

"I love you too. I'll text you with updates."

"Thank you."

"Bye." I hang up and hide my phone in my bag, still attached by the cord of the charger. Then I pull out my iPad and open up my last illustration. If I'm going to be stuck here for the next few hours then I might as well occupy myself.

DECEMBER 25, 2019

It's odd waking up in an airport.

Then again, I'm not sure if I actually fell asleep. It was more like micro-napping: waking up every thirty minutes or so to readjust my spot in the uncomfortable seats at the gate. At least they're big enough that I could curl up into them, though it's done a number on my back.

And Ryder is still here.

Him getting lost in the airport must've just been a really weird dream.

"Ugh," I stretch my arms high in the air and yawn. "Morning, buddy."

Ryder peeks up at me from the floor.

"You want to go to the bathroom?"

His tail starts to wag.

"Good, I can brush my teeth while we're up." I look around at the crowd of people, some of them still sleeping, others awake now, all of us miserable.

Then it hits me.

It's Christmas.

Fuck.

I let Ryder pee, and I drag him to the smaller gender-neutral bathroom with me so I can brush my teeth and wash my face.

I guess I failed.

I didn't get Ryder to Nathan by Christmas. I didn't make it home and Nathan's going to wake up in his bed alone, and I'll be on the other side of the country. Maybe it's dramatic, but I feel like crying.

I didn't want to mess this up.

I didn't want to fail.

I didn't want to miss our first Christmas together.

The intercom in the bathroom starts playing an Ariana Grande cover of a Christmas song and it just makes me want to cry even harder.

"Sorry, Ryder," I pat his head. "It's going to be a bit longer before you see your dad."

He doesn't even know what's going on. He just smiles at me, his tongue hanging out of his mouth. I feel bad, I should've saved his water bowl so he could have something, but I didn't expect that we'd still be here.

I didn't even buy any food at any of the shops before they closed last night. All I've got is a granola bar that one of my roommates made me pack just in case I'd need it.

Guess this proves them right.

"I really thought we'd be able to make it, Ryder," I tell him, chewing the dry granola.

Now I really wish I had a water bottle. I'll have to look around for a fountain, or maybe the airport staff passed some out during the night.

We both walk back to the gate. They still haven't cancelled the flight, but they stopped updating the time, so according to the screen, we departed at 4:30 in the afternoon yesterday.

If only.

"Hello," I say to the flight attendant. She's different from any of the ones working yesterday—maybe it's a good thing

42

if she could make it to work today? Or maybe she was stuck here overnight too. "I was wondering if you had an update on the flight?"

"Unfortunately, we don't; the temperatures got below freezing last night, so all the melted snow froze back over, and then the snow started coming down hard again."

"Oh, well... thanks."

"They're working hard to clear the runways. It's a bit complicated, but basically once we clear off enough snow and a plane takes off, we have to do it all over again. It's falling that fast. Rinse and repeat."

"Really? That's great."

"Yep." She gives me a flat smile. "The queue is expected to be a long one, as we've got about thirty flights and one functioning runway, so I wouldn't get your hopes up."

"Got it..." And just like that, I'm back at rock bottom again.

"We're prepared to offer vouchers for future flights. Do you live in Raleigh?"

"My sister does."

"Do you want to book a flight at a different date? I could help with that."

I look out the window behind her, there's a plane landing in the distance, on the other side of the airport. I don't like the way it looks as it skids to a stop, and I'm already pretty skeptical of normal flights.

Maybe I should just cancel.

Nathan's surprise is ruined, and there's no way I'm making it back to him any time soon.

"Yeah..." I tell them. "I'll just do the voucher."

"We do apologize for the inconvenience," she tells me, typing something quickly.

"It's okay... not your fault."

I take the vouchers—one for me, one for Ryder—and tuck them into my pocket.

"Is it okay if I hang out here while I wait for my ride?"

"Um… sure?" Her eyebrows furrow and she's looking at me like I've grown a second head. I guess that's not a thing normal, non-anxious people do.

I find the same seat that my butt has become acquainted with over the last 24 hours and dial Hannah's number.

"You're still at the airport?" Hannah doesn't even let me say hello.

"Yeah."

"Why didn't you call me? I'd assumed your plane left during the night or something."

"Hannah… please don't. Not right now."

"Benji…"

"I just…" I can feel it, the heat behind my eyes, the ache in my jaw. "I just wanted to get home to him, I wanted this to be a surprise, I wanted it to be special."

"Ben… I know you had this grand romantic plan, but it's just not safe. It'd be better if you came home."

"I know…"

"We'll leave now to come and get you."

"Okay."

"We'll call when we're close. You just wait inside where it's warm."

"Yeah."

"Love you."

"Love you too."

I end the call first—I can't talk to her anymore. I just want to cry. I want to scream, and I want to know how I could be so stupid to think that I could actually pull this off. All of this hiding and waiting and lying to Nathan, and for what?

44

For nothing.

I'm so mad at myself.

I feel the cold press of a nose against my skin as Ryder gets in closer, resting his head on my lap.

"Hey, boy…" I pet him, wiping my eyes with my other hand. "Sorry, I'm just angry."

Now if he could talk, maybe he could tell me it'd all be okay, and Nathan won't be angry with me for missing our first Christmas together, or angry with me for hiding everything from him.

God, I hate this.

I pull my phone back out and go to my recent calls.

I should just tell Nathan the truth and apologize; he'll understand, he always does. I'm not even afraid of what he'll say, but my anxiety is getting to me. It's telling me that he'll yell and be angry and maybe break up with me over this.

None of that is true.

Not a bit.

But anxiety makes liars out of the best of us.

I really wish there was a laser some doctor could blast my brain with to make it different. Even the medication can only do so much. It isn't a permanent fix. Just a buffer, something to help ease me.

But when the anxiety gets this bad… it doesn't really work. I should probably talk to Dr. Taylor about that.

"We'll get you back to Hannah's house," I tell Ryder. "Chill for a few days and it'll be fine."

Ryder just stares at me. He has no idea what's going on.

He's just happy to be here.

I got to my recent calls, and tap Nathan's name. The phone rings and rings and rings.

But there's no answer.

It's 11:00, Nathan would usually be up by now, even if he doesn't have class or work. He's such an early bird, out of bed at 8:00 on the dot, every single morning.

Including the weekends.

Maybe he just set his phone down?

Or maybe he saw my name and didn't want to talk to me...

I dial him again.

Ring, ring, ring.

No answer.

I stare at my screen, my mouth open. It's nothing—it's not a big deal—but everything around me is crumbling. The last thing I needed was for my boyfriend to ignore me. He isn't... he isn't ignoring me. That's what I have to tell myself.

But there's that awful voice in the back of my brain that tells me he is, that I'll get back to California and all the things I've left in his dorm will be in a box, and he'll come back to my apartment to get all his things.

That isn't true.

It isn't.

Why can't my brain just be different?

The call goes to voicemail again, and I want to throw my phone against a wall. I just want this day to end, and it's not even noon.

It needs to be over.

Now.

Ryder perks up from his spot on my lap, and it's like the whole thing plays out in slow motion. He starts to move and I realize that I didn't tie his leash to the seat again. So the moment he realizes that he's free, he bolts.

I reach to stop him, but the leash just barely escapes me, dragging behind Ryder as he runs.

"Ryder! Stop!"

He doesn't listen to me, though; he just keeps running.

"Ryder! Please!"

You'd think that someone—anyone—would help me out, but no. People just stare as I chase this dog through the airport.

Thanks, I guess.

Just throw one more thing at me universe. Please, I'm begging you. I'm stuck in an airport on Christmas, with a dog on the loose, and an upset boyfriend back in California. Just one more thing.

Please.

Well, the universe giveth.

Because I don't notice the wet floor sign until it's too late.

My foot catches the floor the wrong way just as I see Ryder vanish around the corner, and next thing I know, it feels like the floor is being yanked out from underneath me. I try to catch myself, but I just end up falling on my butt, and the sharp pain shoots through my entire back.

I don't dare look up at all the eyes that are now focused on me. The airport was quiet before, but now that silence feels louder than ever. I just want to die.

I want to curl up, cry, and completely vanish into the ether. I want the floor to swallow me whole, to blink out of existence.

This was so stupid.

I'm so stupid.

I should've just stayed with Hannah yesterday morning; it would've saved me so much time and grief.

Goddammit.

I wipe the corners of my eyes, not daring to look up for even a second. But then I hear a familiar clacking noise, like the sound of paw against the tiled part of the airport floor. A cold nose pokes me, digging under my hand, begging me to give it pets.

"Ryder..." I whisper. "You had me worried sick."

"Yeah, I caught him around the corner," a voice says.

Wait.

I don't want to look up, because I don't know if this is real, or if it's just some cruel trick my brain is pulling.

"Ben? Baby, are you okay?"

When I do dare to glance past my arms, I see a set of feet next to Ryder's paws, a familiar pair of worn out yellow Converses that I painted sunflowers on a few weeks ago. My eyes trace up those long, long legs, and I see so many other things I recognize: his warm brown skin, his glowing smile, those freckles, the brown eyes that I fell in love with.

"Hey..." Nathan squats down to my level. "What's wrong?"

That's the straw that breaks the camel's back.

I start sobbing.

Because he's here.

Nathan is actually here, right in front of me. This isn't my imagination—this isn't some weird combination of chemicals in my mind.

He's right in front of me, he's real.

He's real...

"Are you okay? Did your fall break anything?" Nathan gets down on his knees, checking the palms of my hands. "Nothing hurts?"

Except my pride.

And my ass a little bit.

"No, no." I throw my arms around his neck and pull him in as close as I possibly can. Nathan goes tense at first, but then he finally relaxes, hugging me back. "You're here," I say.

"I am. I'm here." He rubs small circles in my back. Nathan isn't a magic cure for the anxiety—that'd be ridiculous—but I do feel so much easier when he's here, when he's touching me. Playing with my hair or holding my hand.

I feel grounded.

I feel real.

When I've mostly recovered from my breakdown, Nathan and I take Ryder to a more secluded spot, away from the crowds and prying (and unhelpful!) eyes.

"What are you... how did you even... what's going on?" I have so many questions that my mouth can't keep up with my brain. "I can't believe that you're here, I can't— How did you even get a flight, I—"

"Take it slow," Nathan holds me. "You're going a thousand miles an hour."

"What are you doing here?"

"Well, a little birdie told me all about your surprise and how you were stuck in the airport."

"Mariam?"

"Mariam." Nathan laughs.

"I can't believe they told."

"Well... babe, it wasn't all them."

"When did you know?" I ask.

"I figured you were up to something when you answered my call and I could totally see a plane in the background."

"You saw that?"

He nods. "Mariam told me what was going on when I asked. They told me about the delays, and I didn't want to spend Christmas without you, so..."

"How did you even get here?"

"We just landed a few minutes ago, I figured you either had to still be stuck here or at Hannah's. I was actually about to call you when—" Nathan looks at Ryder. "He happened."

"I can't believe they let you land."

"Me either, but I guess the number of flights coming into a snowstorm is smaller than the ones trying to go out." He laughs, and it's like music to my ears. I don't care if it's only been two days since we've seen each other, I missed him so much.

"I tried to call you," I say. "I was so scared that you were mad at me for missing Christmas."

"My phone was on airplane mode."

"Right..."

God, I feel foolish.

"Sorry your plan was spoiled," he says.

"I really wanted it to be special. I wanted to take him to your dorm and surprise you."

Nathan's hand finds my hair, brushing it away from my face. "It's the thought that counts. And I've got my two special people here, so I'd count that as a win."

I look down at Ryder. "He must've smelled you or something."

"Yeah..." Nathan sighs. "I didn't even realize it was Ryder at first. I almost started running from him."

"He's not that scary."

"Scary enough to freak me out when he was sprinting at me."

"I'm sure he's very sorry."

"I'm sure he is." Nathan takes my hand.

"I, um... I'm really sorry that I lied to you, about missing Christmas."

He rolls his eyes. "Are you actually worried about that?"

I give him a guilty look.

"You were going to fly two days before Christmas to get my dog to come and surprise me..."

"You aren't mad at me, right?"

"Why would I be mad at you?"

"I was worried."

"Hey," Nathan's hand on my cheek guides my gaze to his. "Your brain is being mean, remember that."

"I know."

"I love you Benjamin De Backer." He leans in, kissing my forehead. "I love you and your mean brain."

"I love you too."

My heart still feels heavy in my chest, and I'm sure I could vomit from the anxiety if I think about it hard enough. But at least Nathan is here to hold my hand through all of it. I don't really know what I'd do without him.

We kiss again, on the lips this time. And I don't care how many times we've kissed over the last half a year; I'll never get tired of kissing Nathan Allan. It isn't fireworks every single time—sometimes they're long or short, chaste or passionate, on the lips, on the cheek, on the forehead.

Whatever Nathan wants to give me, I'm prepared to take.

My phone starts to ring in my pocket, because of course it does. I don't want to pull away from Nathan, but I know that I have to.

"One second?" I look at him, and he's smiling just as bright as before. "Hello?"

"Hey Benji, we made it. They've gotten the highways cleaned up pretty well, so it didn't take as long as we thought."

"Oh, wow… that's fantastic."

"If you tell me you're on a plane to California I will actually buy a ticket right now and go murder you myself."

"No, no. I'm still here."

"Good, because Thomas bought another chicken, and he's demanding a Christmas dinner do-over." I hear her mutter something. "Yeah, we can wait here, I think. Come on out,

Ben, we're in the pick-up zone."

"Okay, I'll be there..." I look at Nathan. "Um, would it be possible if someone else joined us for dinner?"

"What, did you meet a friend at the airport?"

"Something like that." I smile at him.

"Well bring them with you, weirdo. And hurry up, it's cold out here!"

Hannah ends the call, and I slip my phone back into my pants pocket. "So, do you want to go have dinner at Hannah's?"

Nathan smiles at me, showing off those handsome dimples. He grabs his own bag, and Ryder's leash. "Sure thing. Let's go."

Of course, with Nathan back, we drag his parents over to Hannah's house for dinner. There isn't really enough food for six people, but we make it work with leftover pizza added to the mix.

It's a bit of a strange combination.

But then again, none of us really care, so long as we're together.

It's just nice to have Nathan here with me, our families beside us. I was so afraid that I'd never get this again, that I'd never think of Christmas the same way I used to, not with everything that happened.

God, that feels like a lifetime ago.

When dinner is done, we crowd into the living room for Christmas movies. Nathan brought his Switch, so we manage to convince everyone to play a few rounds of Mario Kart and Mario Party. Mrs. Allan busts out the UNO cards that she carries with her no matter where she goes.

Apparently, there's always time for a game of UNO. Nathan's parents eventually make their way home, and we're not done cleaning until after midnight, so Hannah and Thomas go upstairs to bed before us.

"You two don't stay up too late, okay?" Hannah says, turning off the lights in the kitchen.

"We won't."

And now, it's just me and Nathan on the couch, watching the Charlie Brown Christmas special on a low volume. Nathan's laptop's playing one of those endless loops of the fireplaces and the only other lights are the ones from the Christmas tree.

This feels nice.

This feels right.

"I'm glad that you're here," I say. "Even if you're only here because my plan was ruined."

Nathan pets Ryder's head. He hasn't left Nathan's side since we got here. Even the door to the bathroom was no match for Ryder's love for Nathan.

"It was a good plan, I'll give you that."

"It would've been better if I'd been able to pull it off." I lay my head on his shoulder.

"Maybe, but it's the thought that counts. Besides," he sighs, "I'm sure we had more fun tonight than we would've alone in my dorm room."

"You're probably right."

"And now you can say you've spent the night at an airport!"

"Yeah... I don't think I'll be telling anyone about that story."

"Probably for the best." Nathan lays his head back. "I must say, Benjamin, I think that you've won our first Christmas."

"There's no winning Christmas," I tell him, then I think about what he said. "Wait, does that mean you got me something?"

Nathan stares at me, like he can't believe I'd ask something like that. "You're serious?"

"What? I didn't want to assume." I pull my body in close.

"You didn't have to get me anything."

Nathan glares even harder, as if that's possible. "I can't believe you." He manages to get Ryder off his lap, but Ryder isn't even bothered—he's so worn out that he just keeps right on sleeping. Nathan vanishes into the kitchen, coming back with his backpack.

"I wanted to do something special. I thought that jewelry might be too much, and also you don't really wear jewelry... Clothes didn't feel right, and I didn't know what art supplies you might need."

"I'm sure it's perfect," I tell him.

"Remember when I helped my dad clean the attic at Thanksgiving, and you wanted to help but I said you couldn't?" He takes a seat across from me on the coffee table.

"Yeah..."

"Well I'm sure you figured it out back then, but that was because we were looking for things."

"What kind of things?"

Nathan pulls out a very messily wrapped gift from his bag. "Open this and find out."

I take the lumpy present. It's slanted, almost like a binder, and there's something that feels very thick about the weight, if that even makes any sense.

"What is it?"

"You kind of have to... open it to find out, ya know?"

"I hate you."

"I love you too."

I rip the wrapping paper carefully. It's the same kind that he used to wrap the very first present that he gave to me, decorated with tiny cartoon Poe Damerons and BB-8s. I tear it away, letting it fall to the floor as I stare at the book in my hands.

"A book," I say.

Nathan rolls his eyes. "Open it."

"I was getting there!"

I almost want to leave it closed just to spite him, but I'm dying to know what's inside. The cover is a photo of baby Nathan, swaddled in a blanket, still in the hospital, probably hours old. There are more pictures as I flip through the book: ones of him in a high-chair or being held by his mom; one of him in a bathing suit standing in an inflatable pool in a backyard; one of him getting an award in elementary school; the ceremony where he went from fifth grade to sixth; an adorable picture of him smiling at the camera with his two front teeth missing.

"It's you."

"It's a book of my baby photos. Well, not really baby photos, but they're pictures that my mom took of me growing up. I thought it'd be nice... or whatever... and I added to it." He rubs the back of his neck, and he won't look at me. "It's probably a bad gift, you know but... yeah."

"Nathan." I say his name softly.

"Yeah?"

"I love it."

"You do?" His smile gets wider, and his cheeks go warm.

"Yeah, I really do."

"Good, because I spent a lot of time copying those photos, because there was no way Mom was letting go of the originals."

"Then that means these are especially mine." I open the book again. Nathan moves from sitting on the coffee table to the spot on the couch beside me.

"That's when I first got Ryder, and when we moved into the house we have now. That's our first Christmas there. That's a family trip back to Colorado."

We keep flipping through the pictures, and with each page, Nathan's growing up in front of my eyes.

"That's my first day of high school," Nathan flips the page. "And this is when I met Meleika." There are a few pictures that Nathan has obviously taken himself, ones that are shaped like they came from a phone screen. "Here's Halloween of my junior year, I was Finn."

I could tell from the jacket.

And then, when we're just a few pages from the end, I'm suddenly met with a picture of myself.

I freeze, staring at it.

I don't remember exactly when this was, but it was obviously only a few months ago. My hair is a bit shorter, my clothes fit better, my face not quite filled out. I'm hunched over a sketchbook, drawing something.

"When is this?"

"Okay, so don't be creeped out," Nathan says. "Remember that day you drew me, when you were tutoring me?"

"Yeah."

"It's from then. You looked so peaceful and… well beautiful. So, I snapped a picture."

I stare down at the page, my name written in cursive just below the picture.

"I hope that it's okay."

"Yeah… it is." I smile at him.

There are a few more pictures: one of us at the art gallery, before the night turned to disaster; one of us on the roof, the night he missed prom; one of me from across an airport terminal when he picked me up after our big move; one of him on his first day of college (I'd made him take that one, for myself and Mrs. Allan).

And then the book is done.

Eighteen years of a life contained in a single book that he made for me.

"I love it, Nathan."

"I'm glad," he smiles at me. "I love you, Benjamin DeBacker."

"I love you too."

He takes my hand, and he feels like home.

"Merry Christmas."

ACKNOWLEDGEMENTS

So, here we are! A continuation of Ben and Nathan's story. Ever since *I Wish You All the Best* first came out, I've had readers clamoring for more. The only problem was, I never wanted to write a story that I didn't believe organically fit into Ben and Nathan's narrative. I tried for months to come up with a plot, and even made it far with a few ideas. But none of it ever felt right. And I never wanted to give my readers a story that I myself didn't believe in.

There was one idea though. A small story, set over Christmas, where Ben is attempting to get Ryder to Nathan. For an entire year this story stuck with me, somewhere in the back of my mind. And I sort of have a personal rule, if a story sticks with you for at least a year, then you should tell it, however you can.

And now you have it, this weird little idea that I've kept in my head for awhile now, and always wanted to tell, but never knew exactly the right way to do so. While I probably could've started on a Christmas-themed story sooner than late October, I've spent the last few weeks working alongside hardworking dedicated people making sure this story was available to everyone in the best possible way. Of course this team is a lot smaller, but there are still people to thank.

My best friend Hương, whose skills with editing, typesetting, and design really made this feel like our own little creation.

Of course Alice Oseman, for the amazing artwork you see on the cover of this book.

My friends Crystal, Sina, Nina, and Christine for reading the early (almost) finished version of this story and lending your kind words to make this feel extra real.

My agent, Lauren Abramo, who made sure I didn't get in trouble for writing this and for offering her support and guidance, not just for this project, but for every project we've worked on! I don't think I could've asked for a better agent, and I'm so grateful that we get to work together. And my editors David Levithan and Jeffrey West who believed in Ben and Nathan's story, and all the future stories I want to tell.

I can also take this time to finally thank the entire team from Scholastic and IReadYA for their hard work on *I Wish You All the Best*, thank you all for everything you've done.

And finally, to you, my readers. You've made the last year and a half one of the best experiences I could've ever imagined. You've loved and celebrated and cried for Ben and Nathan. You all believed in a quiet little story about a non-binary teenager facing trauma, finding a new family and first love, and you have my eternal gratitude for that.

You're amazing.

I wish you all the best,

Mason

ABOUT THE AUTHOR

Born and raised in a small North Carolina town, Mason Deaver is an award-nominated, bestselling author and designer living in North Carolina.

Besides writing, they're an active fan of horror movies and video games.

Made in the USA
Middletown, DE
03 December 2021

54092314R00036